Whoa, Baby, Whoa!

For Junior, who inspired this book
—G. N.

For Bram, Baby, Bram
All my love
—Ellie x

First published in Great Britain in July 2011 by Bloomsbury Publishing Plc
Published in the United States of America in February 2012
by Bloomsbury Books for Young Readers
www.bloomsburykids.com

For information about permission to reproduce selections from this book, write to
Permissions, Bloomsbury BFYR, 175 Fifth Avenue, New York, New York 10010

Library of Congress Cataloging-in-Publication Data
Nichols, Grace.
[No, baby, no!]
Whoa, baby, whoa! / by Grace Nichols ; illustrated by Eleanor Taylor. — 1st U.S. ed.
p.   cm.
Summary: A baby finally finds something to do that does not make everyone in the family tell him "No."
ISBN 978-1-59990-742-0 (hardback)
[1. Babies—Fiction.] I. Taylor, Eleanor, ill. II. Title.
PZ8.3.N5249Wh 2012   [E]—dc22   2010048953

Art created with watercolor
Typeset in P22 Garamouche
Book design by Claire Jones
Printed in China by Toppan Leefung Printing Ltd., Dongguan, Guangdong
2 4 6 8 10 9 7 5 3 1

All papers used by Bloomsbury Publishing, Inc., are natural, recyclable products
made from wood grown in well-managed forests. The manufacturing processes
conform to the environmental regulations of the country of origin.

Whoa, Baby, Whoa!

Grace Nichols

illustrated by Eleanor Taylor

BLOOMSBURY

NEW YORK BERLIN LONDON SYDNEY

Whatever I do,
wherever I go,
it's always the same old cry:

"Whoa,
Baby,
whoa!"

Creeping to the kitchen
to see what's cooking

Up goes the gate
and Daddy comes
running . . .

"Whoa, Baby, whoa!
Hot things can burn you in the kitchen."

Tearing up the newspaper

Chewing bits in my mouth

Along comes Mommy
and scoops it out
with a shout . . .

"Whoa, Baby, whoa!
Newspapers are for reading,
not for eating."

Climbing
up Grandpa
like a
mountaineer

Grabbing
at those glasses
he likes to wear . . .

"Whoa,
Baby, whoa!
You sure like doing that
but without my glasses
I'm blind as a bat."

Reaching
for a book

High on
a shelf

Over comes my sister,
as if I need some help . . .

"Whoa, Baby, whoa!
You'll pull that shelf
down on yourself."

Having fun in the tub
with my rubber duck

Making big splashes
that go over the top . . .

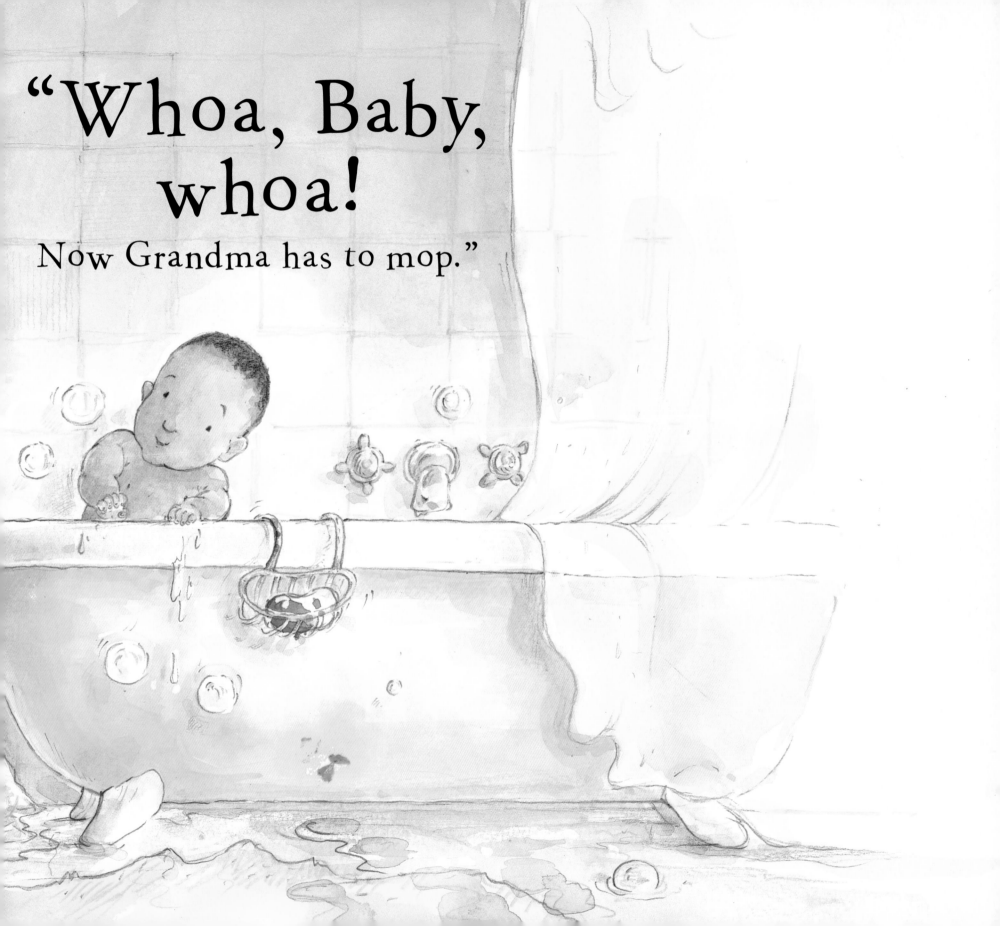

"Whoa, Baby,
whoa!
Now Grandma has to mop."

Sitting
in my
high chair

Playing
with my food

Again comes Mommy
to feed me with a spoon . . .

"Whoa, Baby, whoa!

Have a taste.
Mashed potato isn't
for your face."

Oh, whatever I do,
wherever I go,
it's always the same old cry:

So today
I'll try something new
with myself.

One step, two steps
. . . maybe more?

Look, I'm walking across the floor!

And no one is saying,
"Whoa, Baby,
whoa!"

Everyone's smiling and clapping.

"Go, Baby, go!"   "Go, Baby, go!"